Most Bunnies Hop, But Some Bunnies Fly

Written by Ammar Habib
Illustrated by Carlos Lemos

ISBN 978-1-61225-485-2

Published by Mirror Publishing
Fort Payne, Alabama 35967

Printed in the USA.

This story is for all the children who have ever felt a little different. Remember, just like Nemo, you can fly!

And a special thank you to my sweet mother for teaching her own Nemo how to fly.

About the Author

Ammar Habib is an award-winning author from Lake Jackson, Texas. He enjoys crafting stories that are entertaining and inspiring. You can learn more about Ammar at:

www.ammarahsenhabib.com

Nemo the Bunny was a little bunny, but he faced a big problem. Nemo could not hop! He knew that dogs go *woof, woof, woof.* He knew that cheetahs go *run, run, run.* He knew that bunnies go *hop, hop, hop.* But for some reason, he was different.

He ran like the other bunnies. He walked like them, too. He even looked like them. But he could not hop like them no matter how hard he tried.

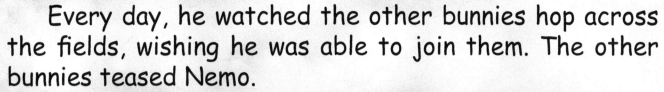

Every day, he watched the other bunnies hop across the fields, wishing he was able to join them. The other bunnies teased Nemo.

Sometimes, they asked him, "Why can't you hop like us, Nemo?" Other times, they asked him, "Why are you so different, Nemo?" It made him very sad when they said those things.

One day, Nemo visited Mr. Owl. Mr. Owl was very wise and knew the answer to any question. "Hello, Mr. Owl," Nemo said. "I cannot hop like the other bunnies. What should I do?"

Mr. Owl thought long and hard. "Well, Nemo," he replied. "If you cannot hop, then maybe you should try finding something else that you can do."

Nemo decided to do just that. He first went to the monkeys. Nemo thought they were so cool as he watched them climb up the trees and hang from the high branches.

Seeing the monkeys have fun, Nemo wished to be as happy as them. But when he tried to climb the trees, he just could not do it no matter how many times he tried.

Not being able to climb the trees made Nemo a little sad. He went back to Mr. Owl. "Mr. Owl," he said. "I can't hop like the bunnies or climb trees like the monkeys. What should I do?"

Mr. Owl again thought long and hard. "Well," he replied. "Maybe you should try something else and find what you can do."

Following Mr. Owl's advice, Nemo chose to visit the fishes that lived in the pond. Just like the bunnies and monkeys, the fishes looked very happy as they swam up and down the pond.

He wanted to be just like them. Nemo tried to go into the water. But instead of swimming, he went straight down with a loud splash! Nemo raced out of the pond all wet and scared.

"I can't hop like the bunnies, climb like the monkeys, or swim like the fish," Nemo said to himself. "What can I do?"

It looked like there was nothing that he could do right. Nemo became very sad as he kept watching all the bunnies *hop, hop, hop* from far away. They sounded so happy as they laughed and played in the fields. But the more Nemo watched them, the sadder he felt.

Winter soon arrived, and snow began falling from the sky. Nemo enjoyed going onto the piles of snow and sitting by himself. One day, he fell asleep on top of a big pile of snow. Nemo was so tired from playing that he slept for a long time. When he woke up, the snow had melted, and he was on a branch high up from the ground!

Nemo became scared. He had never been on a tree branch before. He covered his eyes with his paws and began flapping his big ears. He flapped and flapped and flapped his ears as fast as possible.

When Nemo finally opened his eyes, he was no longer on the branch. Instead, he was flying in the air high above the branch! Nemo could not believe it. How could a bunny fly? The more he thought about it, the faster he flapped his ears and the higher he went.

Nemo was so excited! He was now happier than all the bunnies, monkeys, and fish. He finally knew what he could do. He flew between the trees. He soared high into the sky. He glided above all the other animals.

The entire forest heard his laughter. Soon, all the other bunnies did not want to hop anymore. Instead, they wanted to fly just like Nemo.

Sometimes, bunnies are not meant to hop. Sometimes bunnies—just like people—are meant to fly.

The End

CPSIA information can be obtained
at www.ICGtesting.com
Printed in the USA
BVHW012324090223
658260BV00014B/291